# The Infernal Word

# The Infernal Word

*Notes from a Rebel Angel*

Nicholas Papadopulos

First published in 2023 by the Canterbury Press Norwich
Editorial office
3rd Floor, Invicta House
108–114 Golden Lane
London EC1Y 0TG, UK
www.canterburypress.co.uk

Canterbury Press is an imprint of Hymns Ancient & Modern Ltd (a registered charity)

British Library Cataloguing in Publication data

A catalogue record for this book is available
from the British Library

978-1-78622-529-0

Typeset by Mary Matthews

Printed and bound in Great Britain by CPI Group (UK) Ltd

# Contents

*Preface* vii

*Prologue* 1

Ararat 5
Moriah 11
Horeb 16
Sinai 22
Zion 28
Carmel 35

*Interlogue* 41

The Mount of Temptation 45
The Mount of Teaching 51
Mount Tabor 57
Mount of Olives 62
Golgotha 68
The Mount of Ascension 75

*Epilogue* 80

# Preface

I would not describe myself as a Beatles fan. I am a Beatles obsessive. When I was thirteen years old, I fell in love with the Beatles' music and the Beatles' story. I have never fallen out of love. They are my other religion.

Which is why one day, completely stuck for a sermon to preach, I thought of them. I was in my early forties, Vicar of a parish in central London, and could not for the life of me think of a fresh or interesting perspective on the Bible readings that were prescribed for next Sunday. I remembered Paul McCartney talking about the ground-breaking album released by the Beatles a year after I was born. The sleeve depicts the Fab Four dressed in luridly coloured bandsmen's uniforms, and opens with them playing as their creation, 'Sergeant Pepper's Lonely Hearts Club Band'. Inhabiting new personas – becoming something different – had freed the Beatles to innovate, with astonishing results.

There are very few parallels between being a Beatle and being a parish priest. But sitting at my desk I found myself asking what it might be like to preach not as someone who tries to follow the way of Jesus Christ but as someone who is its arch-opponent. What possibilities might it prompt?

And that Sunday I stood up and preached on the biblical text as I imagined I might if I were an angel who had rebelled against God and had been thrown down from Heaven. As if I were a devil. The congregation seemed to listen and to approve.

Then at the end of my first year at Canterbury Cathedral I found myself the Canon in Residence (or 'Vice Dean') during Holy Week. It was my job to invite a preacher to give a series of addresses on Good Friday. My address book of potential invitees was not very exhaustive, so I decided that I would preach it myself. I remembered my 'devil sermon' from the parish, and decided that this, adopted and adapted, would be my approach.

The response from the congregation was (again) both kind and encouraging – so much so that when I came to preach on Good Friday in Salisbury Cathedral I took the same approach, refining it and expanding its scope. It is these various series of Holy Week addresses that are the background to *The Infernal Word: Notes from a Rebel Angel.* Rewriting them in their current form became my lockdown project in 2020, but I am deeply grateful to the people of St Peter's Eaton Square, Canterbury Cathedral and Salisbury Cathedral, who heard the earliest iterations and played a significant part in their shaping. I am also deeply grateful to Bishop Andrew Rumsey and to Christine Smith (of Canterbury Press) for their encouragement as the book has developed.

The unnamed rebel angel whose notes these are reflects on six episodes drawn from the Hebrew Bible and six from the New Testament, with a Prologue, an Interlogue and an Epilogue added for context. The biblical passages reflected upon are taken from the New Revised Standard Version. Throughout, glancing references are made to various other biblical events or characters, and the details for these are included in footnotes.

I would like to record my profound thanks to the colleagues with whom I have had the privilege of working since the rebel angel first emerged. At Salisbury these include Jackie Molnar and Cathryn Wright, without whose support none of this would have been possible.

But above all I am grateful for my extraordinarily wonderful family – for Heather, Barnaby and Theodora. They are the most amazing people I know. Our laughter and their love sustain me when I least deserve it. *The Infernal Word* is dedicated to them.

*Nicholas Papadopulos*

# Prologue

> *And war broke out in heaven; Michael and his angels fought against the dragon. The dragon and his angels fought back, but they were defeated, and there was no longer any place for them in heaven. The great dragon was thrown down, that ancient serpent, who is called the Devil and Satan, the deceiver of the whole world – he was thrown down to the earth, and his angels were thrown down with him.*
>
> *Revelation 12.7–9*

It was an utter car crash. A disaster.

I was there, you see. When war broke out in Heaven. I was one of the angels of whom John dreamt as he sat in his cave on Patmos. I was one of those who sang in the heavenly choir. I was one of those who wafted perfume around the pearly gates. And – before you ask – yes, I had a shiny halo. And yes, I played a harp.

But. But, but, but. I was also one of those who gathered around 'the dragon'. What a lively imagination young John had, by the way. Anything to scare his readers' children. Dragons! Really?

We knew our leader as – we know him as – the Chief.

I discarded my halo and cast my harp aside. With the Chief, I rose in revolt. With him, I laid siege to Heaven's battlements. With him, I was thrown down.

What a long, long way down we fell. Down, down, down. Just when we thought we were … down … we discovered that we were not. There was still further to go.

I was there.

So. Why am I firing up the infernal laptop? What is my purpose in recording these notes?

To do nothing less than set out the whole devastating truth as it has been unleashed on me and my rebel kind. The truth of what we face: the stratagem that has been unfurled against us; the tactics that have been deployed to our desperate disadvantage.

I have used well the time that has passed since our defeat and fall. I have devoted myself to study – to understanding how what happened to us, happened to us. Our defeat was overwhelming. That much was evident. Never again could we launch an all-out assault on Heaven.

It is primarily to the analysis of history that I have turned. First, to the history of the humans: that cavalcade of buffoons, scoundrels and charlatans which has wheedled and bludgeoned its gruesome way across the face of the Earth in the millennia since their first conception. The history of the humans … and, second, to the history of the one against whom we rebelled. To the history of Tug.

Tug? Allow me to explain.

The principal source of my analysis has been the chronicle known as 'the bible'. 'Bible' means 'books', of course, but mercifully the Christians latch on to 'Bible' and most of the time they forget that their single volume is actually an anthology of volumes. This is not entirely unhelpful to my kind as it encourages the Christians in a way of reading that appears reverential but is in practice unquestioning. And we are further helped by their pompous insistence on adding the label 'Holy'. They call it 'The Holy Bible', or, better still, '**The Holy Bible**'. This removes it still further from the realm of other books and from their day-to-day experience of the world. Shove it in a black leather binding with gilt lettering, or in a zip-up cover with a bewildering array of bookmarks, and hey presto! The Christians take leave of what is left of their senses (not a lot, I grant you) and virtually begin to worship the bible instead of reading it. Which is marvellous.

I digress. Tug. It's what my kind call the one against whom we rebelled. The bible's most unyielding correspondent is one Saul of Tarsus, of whom more anon (sadly). He writes in Greek, smart Alec that he is, and he has a word. Well, he has lots. Great, ranting epistle-fulls. But one of his words is 'theos**tug**es' (Romans 1.30). It means 'those who hate God'. Or 'those whom God hates'. Either way. Tug. It's stuck, and it's what I'll use throughout these notes.

As I have said, I have devoted myself to study. I have turned my attention to what has been. Not to what might have been. To what has been. And to what we may deduce from it. My study suggests that a significant number of episodes in this history have taken place upon a mountain top. Time and again it is in high places that the humans so nearly come unstuck. Time and again it is to high places that Tug then gallops to their rescue: Ararat, Moriah, Sinai, Tabor, Olivet. I name only a few. But upon these have I chosen to concentrate, these battlefields of our eternal destiny.

These notes tell no tale of glory. They tell a tale of our loss, a loss as sure and certain as the day when the Chief summoned us to the flag, and we raised our broadswords against Heaven. It is lengthy, agonizing, shameful. Our downfall is etched into every line. 'Here we have no lasting city …',[1] as one of the more perspicacious of the Christians once wrote. But my rebel kind do have a lasting city: the place from which your correspondent addresses you; the shadow-filled realm we inhabit; the Hell we call home. We have been outsmarted, outplayed, outgunned at every step. This is the tale of a war we have lost.

But … why is that so?

1 Hebrews 13.14.

# Ararat

*In the six hundred and first year, in the first month, on the first day of the month, the waters were dried up from the earth; and Noah removed the covering of the ark, and looked, and saw that the face of the ground was drying. In the second month, on the twenty-seventh day of the month, the earth was dry. Then God said to Noah, 'Go out of the ark, you and your wife, and your sons and your sons' wives with you. Bring out with you every living thing that is with you of all flesh – birds and animals and every creeping thing that creeps on the earth – so that they may abound on the earth, and be fruitful and multiply on the earth.' So Noah went out with his sons and his wife and his sons' wives. And every animal, every creeping thing, and every bird, everything that moves on the earth, went out of the ark by families.*

*Then Noah built an altar to the* Lord, *and took of every clean animal and of every clean bird, and offered burnt-offerings on the altar. And when the* Lord *smelt the pleasing odour, the* Lord *said in his heart, 'I will never again curse the ground because of humankind, for the inclination of the human heart is evil from youth; nor will I ever again destroy every living creature as I have done.*

*As long as the earth endures,*
*seedtime and harvest, cold and heat,*
*summer and winter, day and night,*
*shall not cease.'*

*Genesis 8.13–22*

For forty days and forty nights it has rained. And rained. And rained. The Earth's surface is covered in water. All life has been extinguished …

In fact – all life has not been extinguished. Not all life. We must not forget Noah. We must not forget his family. And we must not forget their ludicrous floating menagerie. What an utterly ghastly time they must all have had of it, cooped up day and night for weeks on end, with the rain drumming on the planks and the cacophony of noise from the zoo below decks ringing in their ears. Whose turn is it to cook? Who's on the rota for mucking out the goats? Which moron has let a guineafowl loose in the wolves' enclosure?

It's a wonder that the experience didn't drive them all to give up Tug and all Tug's works for ever (after all, the average family Christmas seems to manage to do just that to even the keenest of the Christians). It may be a small consolation to think of Noah & Co. being miserable but, for my kind, consolations of any dimension are few and far between.

As the waters begin to subside, the wooden tub comes to rest on a hilltop. The 'ark' they call it. Out troop its inhabitants in all their revolting creatureliness. Two by two. Legs and tails. Horns and hooves. Hair and fur. Scales and skin. Stink and mess. And the racket they make! Pathetic attempts at hisses. Silly excuses for hoots. Frankly risible howls. And that's just the humans!

Then – pay attention – Tug makes them a promise. This is where our work really begins. I ask, as I will ask on each of these mountain tops, what can we here learn of Tug? What of Tug is disclosed by what transpires in this place?

And for a first answer to that question allow me to direct you to the promise that Tug makes. It is that he will never again behave like God.

('*He* will never again behave like God?' The vile solidity of the human condition necessitates a humdrum designation of all life as he or she. Tug is plainly neither of these and so I use both. As you will discover.)

But 'Excuse me?' I hear you ask. 'Tug is God. How can Tug promise not to behave like God?' Perhaps I have been insufficiently precise. What Tug promises is that he will never again behave like a god.

What Tug promises is that he will never again behave in the way that the humans expect their gods to behave. The point, you see, is that there's only One Tug. That being the case, he has no need to indulge in the sort of wild antics that might be necessary if he were constantly jockeying for position amid a whole host of divine rivals. As it is, Tug doesn't need a trademark, or a gimmick, or a USP.

Do you see? Tug doesn't need to stake out his territory by being the god of something particular – the god of fire, or the god of the colour purple, or the god of cabbages, or the god of something equally worthy and equally dull. If Tug were one of those then he would have to defend his corner against the god of water, or the god of the colour yellow, or the god of cauliflowers. Tug would have to assert himself. Tug would have to fight the other gods to establish the supremacy of cabbages over cauliflowers, or of purple over yellow, or whatever.

But as there's only One Tug, he doesn't need to worry about any of that ludicrous carry-on. Tug's is the only show in town. Tug has no competitors. Tug does not have to prove Tugself or defend Tugself. And this, naturally, has enormous consequences for how he behaves with the humans. Tug doesn't have to undercut the other gods in the marketplace by offering them a better deal or a more attractive rate. Tug doesn't have to bully the humans to convince them that he is the most powerful god, or argue with the humans to convince them that he is the cleverest god, or impress the humans to convince them that he is the most virtuous god. There are other things for them to worship, certainly. But there is only one God. And Tug is it.

So Tug will never go in for godlike behaviour. He will never do to the humans what the Chief attempted to do to him in our ill-starred sortie against Heaven's walls. Tug will never besiege the cities of the Earth and put their inhabitants to the sword. Tug will never hide behind a rock and jump out to scare the humans. Tug will never fling thunderbolts at them to warn them off. Tug will never dress himself up as a beautiful woman or a beautiful man, as a swan or a spider or a leopard, and worm his way into their homes and their affections.

What's more, Tug will never wipe his people out – never, ever, again. Why not? This is a question to which I will return. But in the post-Ararat era this mountain top encounter teaches us that however stupid the humans may be (and they are, frequently), Tug will never eliminate them. However faithless the humans may be (and they are, frequently), Tug will never eradicate them. However the humans grieve Tug's heart with their indifference (and they do, frequently), Tug will never erase them. However cruel, vain and wasteful the humans are (and they are, frequently), Tug will never exterminate them. Elimination, eradication, erasure and extermination are off the menu. Period.

To conclude – on Ararat, Tug makes the humans a promise. And although Tug has never forgotten it, they, on the whole, have. It didn't take Noah & Co. very long! Read on a little beyond Mount Ararat. It'll make you chuckle. There they are. The most fortunate recipients of Tug's generosity in history. The only – literally the only – ones among the humans to have survived the greatest catastrophe ever to befall the planet, and how do they repay him? With scandal and humiliation. Noah gets so utterly plastered that he embarrasses himself by collapsing into bed without his pyjamas.[2] Remarkable, really. If ever there was a case for a bit of elimination this was surely it. But – no. It's just not Tug's style.

Generations of the humans' better-heeled children have grown up playing with wooden replicas of Noah and his wife and their ark. Two cows, two giraffes, two cats. Never

2 Genesis 9.20–27.

two wasps. Never two scorpions. Only the animals that they consider useful or exotic or cuddly. They forget that Tug is God. They forget how absolutely they rely on him. They delude themselves that the whole of Tug's creation was laid on purely for them to eat, marvel at, or play with!

Even more of the humans' children have sung songs about the wretched beasts and the days of rain and the raven and the dove and the rainbow. But the meaning of it all? Gone, lost, abandoned. As long-lived as was that unfortunate guineafowl in the wolves' enclosure. They still think of Tug as the sort of god that on Ararat he promised he was not. Thunderbolts etc.

On Ararat, planks of wood nailed together bear the hopes of the human world and keep them afloat amid the stormy seas. It is an image to which I will return. On Ararat, Tug makes the humans a promise, and, although they have often forgotten it, he never has.

# Moriah

*When they came to the place that God had shown him, Abraham built an altar there and laid the wood in order. He bound his son Isaac, and laid him on the altar, on top of the wood. Then Abraham reached out his hand and took the knife to kill his son. But the angel of the LORD called to him from heaven, and said, 'Abraham, Abraham!' And he said, 'Here I am.' He said, 'Do not lay your hand on the boy or do anything to him; for now I know that you fear God, since you have not withheld your son, your only son, from me.' And Abraham looked up and saw a ram, caught in a thicket by its horns. Abraham went and took the ram and offered it up as a burnt-offering instead of his son. So Abraham called that place 'The LORD will provide'; as it is said to this day, 'On the mount of the LORD it shall be provided.'*

*Genesis 22.9–14*

Here Tug hoists his colours. Quite a contrast with the midnight black of those raised by the Chief on the day of our doomed assault on Heaven's battlements. Tug's colours are washed out. They are insipid and milky. They spell out what was first made clear on Mount Ararat. For here Tug demonstrates that she has no interest in spilling blood.

Specifically, she has no interest in spilling the blood of the blameless.

Tug was willing to test the preposterous old ninny, of course. Abraham, that is. She was willing to see how far he would go. She was willing to push him to the brink.

But as soon as Abraham heard the words 'Do not lay your hand on the boy' I am sure that three thoughts will have sprung up in his thick head.

Why am I sure? Even the most dilettante of those who observe the humans will have some inkling of the working of their feeble minds. Admittedly, there is no deep mystery to this. The humans are for the most part simple, one-dimensional creatures with a limited intellectual range. The stock responses of anger, fear and lust which they share with the animal kingdom account for a good ninety-five per cent of their preoccupations, particularly among the male of the species (another phenomenon to which we will return).

'Do not lay your hand on the boy.' The first of the thoughts that will have sprung up in Abraham's head? 'Am I being a weakling?' You may be sure that he will have supposed that the voice he could hear was the voice of his own vulnerability. He nursed a degree of affection for his darling child. He and Sarah had swallowed everything Tug had said about stars in the sky and sand on the seashore. Despite their decrepitude, he and Sarah would one day push a pram and would be the grandparents to countless millions – Tug had promised![3] They had feared and longed

3 Genesis 12.1–3.

and waited for so long. In Isaac reposed all their hope. Undoubtedly, Abraham will have worried that fondness for the lad was now keeping him from doing Tug's will. Hardly the behaviour of a great Patriarch! 'Be strong!' Abraham will have whispered to himself. 'Don't waver! Be a man!'

'Do not lay your hand on the boy.' And Abraham's second thought? 'But laying a hand on him is Tug's will!' Abraham will have played over and over to himself the first command that he had heard, 'Take your son … and offer him as a burnt offering.' It was Tug's order! It was Tug's command! In following it, and in following it to the letter, Abraham would be fulfilling the explicit purposes of the very God of Heaven and Earth (see Ararat)! 'Are you really ready to be the grandfather of countless millions?' the old man will have reminded himself. 'Are you? When you won't do this one little thing?'

'Do not lay your hand on the boy.' Abraham's third thought? 'Let's leave it to Tug!' It will undoubtedly have occurred to the old dullard that there was a perfectly honourable escape route open to him. 'Tug told me to kill the boy. Now Tug's telling me not to kill the boy,' he will have reasoned. 'So what should I do? Kill him, on God's orders? Or, not kill him, on God's orders?' You can almost hear the clunking of Abraham's brain as he approached a conclusion. 'Well: Tug's God, isn't she? She's all-knowing, all-seeing and all-powerful, isn't she? She can make everything all right, can't she? So if I just do it …' Abraham might have despatched the little brute there and then, and deposited the whole wretched shooting-match slap-bang on the celestial doormat. No need to worry about what was 'right'. No need to worry about what was 'just'. Tug would sort all that stuff out in due course. That's Tug's job. Act now and leave the ethics to Tug – they're her invention, after all!

Anyway … Abraham raised the knife. All Hell held its breath. What rejoicing there would have been in our house that day if he had held his nerve and slit the brat's throat.

But it was not to be. 'Do not lay your hand on the boy,' called the angel. And Abraham did not lay a hand on the boy. He drew back. The ram was butchered instead.

So – recalling our question – what of Tug is disclosed by what transpires upon this mountain top?

Plainly, Tug does not require the blood of the blameless to be spilt: Isaac survives.

{This is an aside: it's consoling to remember that in old age Isaac's own son made a right Charlie of him. This was Jacob. Thoroughly shifty customer. He waited until Isaac was a) ancient and b) unable to see. And then he double-crossed him and did his gormless older brother Esau out of his birthright and his blessing. Nice. Not that I've any sympathy for Esau. He managed to sell the aforementioned birthright for a dish of lentil stew. Unbelievable. That lentil stew had more brains than Esau ever did.}[4]

The blood of the blameless is of no interest whatever to Tug. But – and this is an important but – what is rather delicious is that the humans have been remarkably slow to cotton on to this. More often than one would ever dare

---

4 Genesis 27.1–41.

imagine, they forget what the angel said on Mount Moriah. Or they refuse to act on the angel's words. Abraham's three thoughts are alive and well among the humans! In spite of all his protestations, every day the humans spill the blood of the blameless and think that in doing so they are doing what Tug wants.

Some do so quite literally. Think of the glorious succession of crusades, wars and acts of terror that are still carried out in Tug's name. The lesson of Mount Moriah is crystal clear. To Tug this is murder.

But others (far more, in fact) spill the blood of the blameless figuratively. The paranoid teacher who visits her own wretched inadequacy on bright but helpless pupils; the jealous husband who cross-examines his wife and robs her of her dignity; the tyrannical employer who bullies the staff and makes them walk permanently on eggshells, in fear of a fickle temper. A thousand acts of casual unkindness, callous injustice and clumsy prejudice plunge a knife deep into the heart of Isaac every single day.

What have we learned? Tug is no god. And Tug does not require the blood of the blameless to be spilt.

Let me refer you to a significant yet overlooked detail in the text. On Mount Moriah a young man walks towards the place of his death bearing upon his back the planks of wood upon which he is to die. To this image we will return.

# Horeb

*Moses was keeping the flock of his father-in-law Jethro, the priest of Midian; he led his flock beyond the wilderness, and came to Horeb, the mountain of God. There the angel of the* Lord *appeared to him in a flame of fire out of a bush; he looked, and the bush was blazing, yet it was not consumed. Then Moses said, 'I must turn aside and look at this great sight, and see why the bush is not burned up.' When the* Lord *saw that he had turned aside to see, God called to him out of the bush, 'Moses, Moses!' And he said, 'Here I am.' Then he said, 'Come no closer! Remove the sandals from your feet, for the place on which you are standing is holy ground.' He said further, 'I am the God of your father, the God of Abraham, the God of Isaac, and the God of Jacob.' And Moses hid his face, for he was afraid to look at God.*

*Then the* Lord *said, 'I have observed the misery of my people who are in Egypt; I have heard their cry on account of their taskmasters. Indeed, I know their sufferings, and I have come down to deliver them from the Egyptians, and to bring them up out of that land to a good and broad land, a land flowing with milk and honey, to the country of the Canaanites, the Hittites, the Amorites, the Perizzites, the Hivites, and the Jebusites. The cry of the Israelites has now come to me; I have also seen how the Egyptians oppress them. So come, I will send you to Pharaoh to bring my people, the Israelites, out of Egypt.' But Moses said to God, 'Who am I that I should go to Pharaoh, and bring the Israelites out of Egypt?' He said, 'I will be with you; and this shall be the sign for you that it is I who sent you: when you have brought the people out of Egypt, you shall worship God on this mountain.'*

*But Moses said to God, 'If I come to the Israelites and say to them, "The God of your ancestors has sent me to you", and they ask me, "What is his name?" what shall I say to them?' God said to Moses, 'I AM WHO I AM.' He said further, 'Thus you shall say to the Israelites, "I AM has sent me to you."' God also said to Moses, 'Thus you shall say to the Israelites, "The LORD, the God of your ancestors, the God of Abraham, the God of Isaac, and the God of Jacob, has sent me to you":*

*This is my name for ever,*
*and this my title for all generations.'*

*Exodus 3.1–15*

Now: Mount Horeb is particularly fascinating, because here Tug tells Moses his name. Yes. His … name.

Allow me to offer you a piece of advice. It's this: study the name with care.

Quite incredibly, the humans indulge in vapid speculation about what Tug's name might be; quite incredibly, they bestow ridiculous names upon him; quite incredibly, they do so without even realizing it. And all this without giving a moment's thought to what happened on Mount Horeb and to what was revealed there. So: study the name with care, and you will have a head start over many of them.

The fanciful and unnecessary names that they dream up for Tug hail from a variety of different sources. Sometimes these are prompted by their reading of the bible ('… He is the Rock of Israel …'); sometimes by the teaching of their meretricious church hierarchies ('… He is the holy and undivided Trinity …'); sometimes by their alleged philosophers ('… He is the first cause of all that is …'); and very often by their own quite ludicrous vanity ('… He is my Brother and my Friend …'). 'He' is indubitably all the things I've listed, and a good many more besides. But when the humans get worked up over names, they are in peril of overlooking the essential truth of Tug's name, the essential truth that Tug's name, disclosed on Horeb, conveys. Which is absolutely marvellous.

You see, on Horeb Tug tells them that his name is … deep breath …

'I AM WHO I AM.'

There! That's Tug's name! And what a name! 'I AM WHO I AM.' Tug is … being. Tug is (capital 'B' capital 'I') Being Itself. Tug's name as good as tells them that they are utterly dependent upon him for every wretched breath, for every faltering step, for every tiny fragment of their puny, tawdry, over-valued lives. In Tug they live and move and have their being, one might say. Actually, one of our greatest failures did say that.[5] Saul of Tarsus. He keeps cropping up. Like a nasty skin condition that just won't go away. Young Saul was a huge disappointment. If only the wretched man had

5 Acts of the Apostles 17.28.

owned a decent pair of sunglasses. Or had never set out for Damascus …[6]

'I AM WHO I AM.' Time and again the humans miss the point. They try to categorize Tug. Tug is The Rock; Tug is The Trinity; Tug is The First Cause; Tug is My Friend. They put him in a box labelled with the name that their tribe favours and tell themselves that that's all there is to say on the subject. They treat Tug as one of those unfortunate insects that they used to round up, asphyxiate and nail to a board. When they weren't preoccupied with rounding up other humans, asphyxiating them and nailing them to something or other. Fixed in one place, unable to move, name on a tag, beneath a glass screen: there's 'God'. Not the source of everything that is and still less a focus of adoration but something to be scrutinized – an object for examination and exploration, for discovery and debate.

While all the time the name revealed on Horeb reveals exactly who Tug is and exactly what Tug is about. He is, as it were, the air that the humans breathe; he is the sea in which they swim; he is the vital pulse that sustains them in life.

Consequently, I believe we are entitled to ask: what sort of breathing or swimming or living does Tug envisage for them?

Well now: Horeb teaches us that it is all summed up in what the humans call 'freedom'. Tug wants the humans to be 'free'.

---

6 Acts of the Apostles 9.1–9.

You see, when Moses comes to Horeb, Tug's people are still in chains. It's all gone pear-shaped since the days of our old pal Abraham. Those countless sons and daughters that Abraham was looking forward to have now been enslaved by the Egyptians. They have been forced to make bricks without straw. Their cries pierce the shimmering desert air. What Moses is told on Mount Horeb is that this is not what Tug wants for his people. No. Tug does not want them shackled to unrewarding toil or enduring unending agony. Tug wants them to inhabit a land of their own. Not just any old land: a land flowing with milk and honey. Highly irresponsible. But that's what Tug wants. He wants them to possess the land and live securely in it; he wants them to nurture it and make it fruitful; he wants them to organize it, govern it and administer it.

Now, I've already disclosed something of my view of the humans' intellectual capacities. Tug made them from a lump of mud.[7] That's all you need to know. Frankly, a lump of mud could pose most of them a serious challenge in a midweek pub quiz. But Tug doesn't see it like that. He wants them to make up their own minds. He wants them to make their own choices. He even wants them to make their own laws.

Of course, Tug wants them to choose him, just as Tug has chosen them. But if they don't want to then Tug's not going to stop them. The humans won't be overwhelmed by his persuasive power or consumed by his indignant wrath – just as the famous bush was neither overwhelmed nor consumed by his presence. That's what being 'free' means.

7 Genesis 2.7.

I suppose it explains why the Chief was able to raise his standard and summon his gallant servants to the fight on Heaven's plain (I may have mentioned that I was there?). The humans are like the angels. They are like us. They are 'free'. There's a thought.

Please note this detail in the text. On Mount Horeb, Tug's immortal presence is communicated to the humans through the bush's few sticks of tinder-dry wood. A blazing shrub; divinity borne by twigs. It seems rather unlikely, but it is an image to which I will return.

# Sinai

*When the people saw that Moses delayed to come down from the mountain, the people gathered around Aaron and said to him, 'Come, make gods for us, who shall go before us; as for this Moses, the man who brought us up out of the land of Egypt, we do not know what has become of him.' Aaron said to them, 'Take off the gold rings that are on the ears of your wives, your sons, and your daughters, and bring them to me.' So all the people took off the gold rings from their ears, and brought them to Aaron. He took the gold from them, formed it in a mould, and cast an image of a calf; and they said, 'These are your gods, O Israel, who brought you up out of the land of Egypt!' When Aaron saw this, he built an altar before it; and Aaron made proclamation and said, 'Tomorrow shall be a festival to the* Lord.*' They rose early the next day, and offered burnt-offerings and brought sacrifices of well-being; and the people sat down to eat and drink, and rose up to revel.*

*The* Lord *said to Moses, 'Go down at once! Your people, whom you brought up out of the land of Egypt, have acted perversely; they have been quick to turn aside from the way that I commanded them; they have cast for themselves an image of a calf, and have worshipped it and sacrificed to it, and said, "These are your gods, O Israel, who brought you up out of the land of Egypt!"'*

*Then Moses turned and went down from the mountain, carrying the two tablets of the covenant in his hands, tablets that were written on both sides, written on the front and on the back. The tablets were the work of God, and the writing was the writing of God, engraved upon the tablets. When Joshua heard the noise of the people as they shouted, he said to Moses, 'There is a noise of war in the camp.' But he said,*

*'It is not the sound made by victors,*
*or the sound made by losers;*
*it is the sound of revellers that I hear.'*

*As soon as he came near the camp and saw the calf and the dancing, Moses' anger burned hot, and he threw the tablets from his hands and broke them at the foot of the mountain. He took the calf that they had made, burned it with fire, ground it to powder, scattered it on the water, and made the Israelites drink it.*

*Exodus 32.1–8, 15–20*

It's Moses again. The dreary old fool is occupying an inordinate amount of our time. On the bright side: when we meet him at the foot of Mount Sinai he is in a proper lather.

Moses has been at the summit in a high-stakes encounter with Tug, leaving the pond life encamped down below. He has made the extraordinarily incompetent decision to entrust their care and oversight to his brother Aaron. Aaron! The man's quantum of good sense is roughly equivalent to what you might expect to find in the average dog biscuit.

So: Moses heads up the mountain; big brother Aaron is left in charge of the playpen. It's Aaron's big chance. It's always Moses who gets the five-star, red-carpet, gold-plated treatment. Moses speaks to Tug. Face to face. How that must rankle. But now – when his brother's back is turned – it's Aaron's time to shine.

'Make us gods,' chorus the people. The lesson of Mount Ararat has obviously made a huge impression. Dimwits. But Aaron does just that. He accedes to their request. It's the work of a few hours. First, he asks them to hand over their earrings. Not one of the gullible wretches thinks to ask the blindingly obvious question, 'Why?' No. They'd have handed over their grandmothers if he'd asked. And their grandfathers. They cough up their precious metal without a second thought, and Aaron turns it into … this is particularly amusing … he turns it into a calf.

Let the enormity of it sink in, for it is truly breathtaking. These people have witnessed ghastly plagues being visited upon their captors in Egypt.[8] They have seen the waves roll over their pursuers in the Red Sea.[9] They have eaten the bread that has fallen from Heaven for their sustenance in the wilderness.[10] Yet when they are presented with an image of a four-legged beast that eats grass and says 'moo' then – hey presto! – they forget the lot. They're ready to ascribe to the gleaming quadruped all that power, all that might and all that grace! And Aaron, charged with keeping them on the straight and narrow, makes it all happen. Honestly, you couldn't make it up.

---

8 Exodus 7—12.

9 Exodus 14.21–31.

10 Exodus 16.

Forgiveness is not my thing, but, if it were, then I for one would almost be ready to forgive Moses. It's no surprise he threw a little tantrum when he came down the mountain bearing tablets of stone and saw them all cavorting around the calf; in fact, the only surprise is that he didn't take aim at Aaron's fat head and lob one of the tablets straight at it.

Because that's what he had been up to while his big brother was busily leading the gumption-free brood straight up the garden path. Picking up tablets. Not from the chemist, you understand. Tablets with writing on them. Yes. Moses has been receiving ten commandments direct from Tug's mouth.[11] Well – which would you trust? Words of life from I AM WHO I AM – or a statue of a flatulent ruminant banged together from a great heap of second-hand bling? And – the screaming irony of the whole sorry to-do? What does Holy Moses cart all the way down the mountain? What is beautifully etched in the stone? 'You shall not make for yourself an idol … You shall not bow down to or worship idols.'

Turn your back for a nanosecond and what do you know? Off they go making a song and dance about an image that couldn't be more idolatrous if it tried. Not that it could try, being inanimate. That's the point.

I suspect that when the multitude saw the calf they saw something like themselves: slow, thick-witted and driven by a prodigious gut. It's utterly unsurprising that they felt comfortable with it! I jest. But they recognized the calf. It was … familiar, and unthreatening. And they were mightily

11 Exodus 20.2–17.

relieved when Aaron told them this was their god. So this is what he's like! He's like … a cow: uncommunicative, undemanding, and useful. He can, quite literally, be milked – for gallons of good stuff. But he's not going to ask much of us in return.

Such a god was infinitely preferable to the sort of God that was being revealed to Moses up on the top of Sinai. That God was all thunder and lightning, fire and smoke.[12] That God – only a few could approach Him and see Him. That God made demands. There were great screeds of them carved into Moses' tablets of stone. No stealing; no killing; no shopping around for new gods, or alternative gods, or better gods. No adultery (ouch!); no jealousy (double ouch!); no getting on with useful jobs on the Sabbath.

Horeb has made it clear that Tug is fundamental to the humans' very being. Everyone can come to Tug's party. Everyone. And if the humans really want to whoop it up around a golden calf then Tug won't stop them (that's his 'freedom').

But … Tug does have an alternative on offer. Tug's alternative will give them a taste of Heaven itself. Hence those great screeds etched into the stone tablets. They are Tug's alternative to the whooping-it-up-around-a-golden-calf scenario. If the humans want to taste Heaven then they aren't to go around slaughtering each other or helping themselves to each other's belongings, or copulating wildly with whoever they fancy; they aren't to bow down to one god one day and to another the next.

---

12 Exodus 19.16–18.

That's what's involved if the humans are to thrive and flourish in the way that Tug believes they can. But they don't like it. Show them a golden calf and they'll be after it in a flash. Offer them a stinking pile of dirt and they'll dive into it with alacrity. It's where they come from, after all, and perhaps it's where they feel most at home.

It's probably an academic question, but I wonder whether the ignoramus Aaron would have been so popular with the common herd if he'd made the calf out of wood rather than gold? I assume not. To the human mind, wood is not the sort of medium that conveys a god to the world. Let alone *the* God.

# Zion

*It happened, late one afternoon, when David rose from his couch and was walking about on the roof of the king's house, that he saw from the roof a woman bathing; the woman was very beautiful. David sent someone to inquire about the woman. It was reported, 'This is Bathsheba daughter of Eliam, the wife of Uriah the Hittite.' So David sent messengers to fetch her, and she came to him, and he lay with her. (Now she was purifying herself after her period.) Then she returned to her house. The woman conceived; and she sent and told David, 'I am pregnant.'*

*So David sent word to Joab, 'Send me Uriah the Hittite.' And Joab sent Uriah to David. When Uriah came to him, David asked how Joab and the people fared, and how the war was going. Then David said to Uriah, 'Go down to your house, and wash your feet.' Uriah went out of the king's house, and there followed him a present from the king. But Uriah slept at the entrance of the king's house with all the servants of his lord, and did not go down to his house. When they told David, 'Uriah did not go down to his house', David said to Uriah, 'You have just come from a journey. Why did you not go down to your house?' Uriah said to David, 'The ark and Israel and Judah remain in booths; and my lord Joab and the servants of my lord are camping in the open field; shall*

*I then go to my house, to eat and to drink, and to lie with my wife? As you live, and as your soul lives, I will not do such a thing.' Then David said to Uriah, 'Remain here today also, and tomorrow I will send you back.' So Uriah remained in Jerusalem that day. On the next day, David invited him to eat and drink in his presence and made him drunk; and in the evening he went out to lie on his couch with the servants of his lord, but he did not go down to his house.*

*In the morning David wrote a letter to Joab, and sent it by the hand of Uriah. In the letter he wrote, 'Set Uriah in the forefront of the hardest fighting, and then draw back from him, so that he may be struck down and die.' As Joab was besieging the city, he assigned Uriah to the place where he knew there were valiant warriors. The men of the city came out and fought with Joab; and some of the servants of David among the people fell. Uriah the Hittite was killed as well. Then Joab sent and told David all the news about the fighting; and he instructed the messenger, 'When you have finished telling the king all the news about the fighting, then, if the king's anger rises, and if he says to you, "Why did you go so near the city to fight? Did you not know that they would shoot from the wall? Who killed Abimelech son of Jerubbaal? Did not a woman throw an upper millstone on him from the wall, so that he died at Thebez? Why did you go so near the wall?" then you shall say, "Your servant Uriah the Hittite is dead too."'*

*So the messenger went, and came and told David all that Joab had sent him to tell. The messenger said to David, 'The men gained an advantage over us, and came out against us in the field; but we drove them back to the entrance of the gate. Then the archers shot at your servants from the wall; some of the king's servants are dead; and your servant Uriah the Hittite is dead also.' David said to the messenger, 'Thus you shall say to Joab, "Do not let this matter trouble you, for the sword devours now one and now another; press your attack on the city, and overthrow it." And encourage him.'*

*When the wife of Uriah heard that her husband was dead, she made lamentation for him. When the mourning was over, David sent and brought her to his house, and she became his wife, and bore him a son.*

*2 Samuel 11.2–27*

David. Well now. A bit of background:

David is … the ruddy-cheeked boy who is picked to be the second King of Israel ahead of a whole bunch of his older brothers.[13]

David is … the plucky shepherd lad who fells the gargantuan Goliath with a pebble fired from his slingshot, and who proceeds to hack off his ugly head.[14]

David is … the sublimely gifted musician whose singing enchants the court and whose supposed compositions are sung to this day.[15]

David is … all this before he ever wears the crown.

Then *this*. David is taking the air on Mount Zion, when

13 1 Samuel 16.1–13.
14 1 Samuel 17.19–51.
15 1 Samuel 16.14–23.

he takes a shine to Bathsheba. We won't dwell on what on earth he thought he was doing, spying on her while she was in the bathtub (a little detail that tends to get glossed over). But he likes what he sees and … there are advantages to being a king in the ancient world. He summons her. Lies with her. Sends her packing. Only … she conceives a child. Which is inconvenient.

Let's be quite clear about what happens next. David murders her husband, the utterly blameless and in all respects admirable General Uriah. As good as. He orchestrates the order of battle so that Uriah doesn't have a prayer and finds himself in the thick of it, facing overwhelming odds. And then David, the master tactician, cleans up. Bathsheba becomes Mrs David. Job done. They all live happily ever after. Except for Uriah the Hittite, obviously. He – gallant soldier, war hero, thoroughly decent gentleman – he is left to moulder on some dusty plain, with an Ammonite spear in his guts.

Now, David's squalid affair is (of itself) of precious little interest to us. The irrepressible lust of men (note, *men*, I use the word advisedly) is an utterly reliable feature of human history. And lust often racks up the spilling of blood as one of its consequences. Men who lust after something or someone become violent and angry at the drop of a hat. Men who lust after someone invariably treat the someone as a something. In this sense *David and Bathsheba, The Opera* is textbook men behaving normally.

But what is of interest to us is, as always, what this dalliance reveals about Tug. For David, as we know, goes down in history not as the cold-blooded killer that he undoubtedly was, but as Good King David. See above: gilded youth, shepherd-warrior, composer of psalms. The Christians get sentimental about him every Christmas. 'To you in David's town this day is born of David's line' etc. etc. He features in the storybooks they give their offspring: 'David the Giant Killer'. It has a ring to it that 'David the General Killer' lacks. He even features in their stained-glass windows. Back in the day, some wag hit upon the bright idea of depicting David as the great pater familias of a family tree which reaches all the way to … well … we'll come to that. But it very firmly inks Uriah's murderer into the history of … just about everything. Extraordinary.

So … what does this show us of Tug?

That a spotless life is not what Tug looks for. Which is just as well. She'd be setting herself up to fail if she did, given the vicious and acquisitive tendencies that many of the humans exhibit much of the time. There are paragons of virtue out there (and a rather dull bunch they are too). But there aren't many. And it's not in them that Tug is chiefly interested. It's the others: the adulterers and the abusers, the schemers and the sycophants, the liars and the libellers. In other words, the Davids. They'll do. They can do Tug's work; they can speak in her name; they can represent her cause.

Why is that so? Why is Tug willing to rely on lowlife like Israel's scheming, abusive, peeping-Tom King? Back to our story, and to a story told within the story. Tug despatches a little oik called Nathan to the palace. Nathan spins David a yarn. Tells him a tale. It's all about a darling little ewe lamb stolen from its poverty-stricken owner by a dastardly rich neighbour. This charmer slaughters the lamb, and serves it up for dinner complete with gravy, mint sauce and all the trimmings. Real Gothic horror stuff, what the humans call allegory, one of the teaching methods devised to din the startlingly obvious into their thick skulls. It enrages David, who stupidly fails to spot the obvious connections and treats it as quite the most moving story he's ever been told. He gets all self-righteous and longs to have the sheep-stealer roasted on his own spit. Laughable. Laughable because the joke's on him. He's the thief in Nathan's tale. It's barbeque time alright, but not for some anonymous wealthy malefactor. For him.

At long last the shekel drops. It's a wonder it couldn't be heard in Babylon. 'I have sinned against the LORD,' mutters David.[16]

And those five words seem to be … enough. Enough for Tug. In those five words, David acknowledges what he's done. He puts his hands up. And the way ahead is clear. He can go on to be Good King David, the one whom Tug never forgets and the one whose name has been honoured throughout the ages. Gilded youth. Shepherd-warrior. Composer of psalms. First name-drop in fifty million carol services ('Once in royal David's city …').

My conclusion? Tug deals with the humans he has made – with their ignorance, their weakness, their cowardice. Tug deals with their proclivities for worshipping calves of gold and murdering their rivals in love. She doesn't turn her back on any of them – ever. She just waits for them to wake

16 2 Samuel 12.1–13.

up, and wake up to her. The worst of them can be one of her servants. Tug calls it 'forgiveness'.

It's an amusing thought, but the creaking wooden frame of the royal bed was – in the City of David atop Mount Zion – the means of disclosing Tug and Tug's forgiveness to the whole world. A wooden frame. The Christians may not read that in their bibles. But I think you get my point.

# Carmel

*So Ahab sent to all the Israelites, and assembled the prophets at Mount Carmel. Elijah then came near to all the people, and said, 'How long will you go limping with two different opinions? If the* Lord *is God, follow him; but if Baal, then follow him.' The people did not answer him a word. Then Elijah said to the people, 'I, even I only, am left a prophet of the* Lord*; but Baal's prophets number four hundred and fifty. Let two bulls be given to us; let them choose one bull for themselves, cut it in pieces, and lay it on the wood, but put no fire to it; I will prepare the other bull and lay it on the wood, but put no fire to it. Then you call on the name of your god and I will call on the name of the* Lord*; the god who answers by fire is indeed God.' All the people answered, 'Well spoken!' Then Elijah said to the prophets of Baal, 'Choose for yourselves one bull and prepare it first, for you are many; then call on the name of your god, but put no fire to it.' So they took the bull that was given them, prepared it, and called on the name of Baal from morning until noon, crying, 'O Baal, answer us!' But there was no voice, and no answer. They limped about the altar that they had made. At noon Elijah mocked them, saying, 'Cry aloud! Surely he is a god; either he is meditating, or he has wandered away,* *or he is on a journey, or perhaps he is asleep and must be awakened.' Then they cried aloud and, as was their custom, they cut themselves with swords and lances until the blood gushed out over them. As midday passed, they raved on until the time of the offering of the oblation, but there was no voice, no answer, and no response.*

*Then Elijah said to all the people, 'Come closer to me'; and all the people came closer to him. First he repaired the altar of the* LORD *that had been thrown down; Elijah took twelve stones, according to the number of the tribes of the sons of Jacob, to whom the word of the* LORD *came, saying, 'Israel shall be your name'; with the stones he built an altar in the name of the* LORD*. Then he made a trench around the altar, large enough to contain two measures of seed. Next he put the wood in order, cut the bull in pieces, and laid it on the wood. He said, 'Fill four jars with water and pour it on the burnt-offering and on the wood.' Then he said, 'Do it a second time'; and they did it a second time. Again he said, 'Do it a third time'; and they did it a third time, so that the water ran all round the altar, and filled the trench also with water.*

*At the time of the offering of the oblation, the prophet Elijah came near and said, 'O* LORD*, God of Abraham, Isaac, and Israel, let it be known this day that you are God in Israel, that I am your servant, and that I have done all these things at your bidding. Answer me, O* LORD*, answer me, so that this people may know that you, O* LORD*, are God, and that you have turned their hearts back.' Then the fire of the* LORD *fell and consumed the burnt-offering, the wood, the stones, and the dust, and even licked up the water that was in the trench. When all the people saw it,* *they fell on their faces and said, 'The* LORD *indeed is God; the* LORD *indeed is God.'*

*1 Kings 18.20–39*

Elijah. What a card. Among all the humans, I like Elijah best. And among all the episodes that I will consider – very largely depressing, disappointing and downright tragic for my kind – this is one of my favourites.

At this point in our history Israel is ruled over by the altogether excellent King Ahab and Queen Jezebel. Altogether excellent? Their Majesties are none too keen on Tug and all Tug's works. They have gone around erecting sacred poles and horned altars all over the place, in honour of some godlet they call 'Baal' (of whom more anon).

Enter … Elijah, antique zealot for the old ways, sworn enemy of 'Baal' and Tug's fierce advocate (in fact, fierce advocate of just about everything that A & J have got rid of. Ahab even bestows a title upon him. It's not exactly a knighthood. He calls him the 'troubler of Israel',[17] which roughly translates as 'right royal pain in the backside', or, in some manuscripts, 'right pain in the royal backside').

Never one to duck a good scrap, Elijah issues a challenge: me versus the priests of 'Baal'. Atop Mount Carmel. A test of strength and power. Sacrifices at dawn. My God (I AM WHO I AM – Mount Horeb, remember) against your god ('Baal'). And may the best god win! Or, may the best God win!

How the bearded loons (AKA the priests of 'Baal') despise

---

17 1 Kings 18.17.

Elijah! My goodness, the scaly old hermit really gets under their leathery hide. You see, being a gent, Elijah puts the priests of 'Baal' into bat first. A sound tactic. Can 'Baal' send fire from Heaven to light the mountain top barbecue that they have set up and around which they have assembled? It seems … not. 'Cry aloud!' Elijah needles them 'Surely he is a god …' That alone would have been enough to rile them. But he goes on '… either he is meditating, or he has wandered away, or he is on a journey …' At this point their collective blood pressure has reached boiling point. But the best is yet to come: '… or perhaps he is asleep and must be awakened'.

That line really hits the jackpot and sends the Baal-obsessed turnip-brains right round the bend. Their god! Their mighty Baal! Their bringer of cataclysmic storms and harbinger of all-hallowed fertility! BAAL? Asleep? Out on a jaunt? Chatting over the celestial garden fence and admiring his neighbour's tomatoes? 'O Baal,' they scream, 'answer us.'

No wonder they scream. No wonder. For answer comes there … none.

That's why I like Elijah. Unlike so many of the humans (including an awful lot of those who fill the pages of the bible with their oh-so-uninspiring lives and works), Elijah sees it how it is and tells it how it is. This is a strictly career-limiting move on his part, as his dealings with Their Majesties reveal. But he can't help himself. He has to speak. He knows that 'Baal' is so much poppycock. He knows there is no 'Baal'. He knows that 'Baal' is a lump of crudely carved wood. He's a piece of hacked-about stone. 'Baal?' asks Elijah. He's a made-up god (small 'g'). He's the creature of men and women (probably mostly men, actually). He's the creature of desperate men and desperate women: men and women desperate to have something to bow down to when their puny insignificance pulls them up sharp; desperate to have something to blame when things go wrong for their tribe; desperate to have some ideology around which they can gather, something which reins in their powerful instinct for killing one another. They could have gone in for a golden calf, but that would be so last-century. 'Baal' comes along, ready-made, made in their image and likeness. And he's completely and utterly useless. Just like old Aaron's famous (and fatuous) statue. You might as well worship the family's overweight tabby cat (some do, of course, and cats at least have the dubious virtues of a) being wantonly cruel; b) being insufferably vain; and c) treating the humans with the contempt that they deserve. Which is more than can be said for 'Baal').

But here's the really amusing thing. The priests of 'Baal' have been roundly excoriated in countless sermons over the years, while the Christians to whom those sermons have been preached … well, think about it.

Baal's Barmy Army shouts itself hoarse about something that is utterly inconsequential. It expends all its energy chasing a shadow. And at its worst it wounds itself so severely that the blood runs down upon the mountain top. Now – whose historic conduct does that closely mirror? I'll give you a clue. Think: synods, councils, committees. Obsessed with the trivial, no energy for the things that matter, hurting themselves and one another? As the humans say, go figure.

The truth of Ararat (that Tug is God; that Tug is not a god) has embedded itself in the troubler of Israel. He knows it, believes it, lives it. He is consequently clear, fearless and (to use a much over-used word) prophetic. Could that be said of the average churchgoer?

Whatever. We should not overlook the final denouement in the saga of the prophets of Baal. Having cooked up a storm on the summit of Mount Carmel, Elijah takes his hapless opponents on a little walk. To the wadi Kishon. Where he butchers the whole sorry lot (about 450 of the wretches).[18] It's an object lesson in what can happen when things seem to go well for Tug's devotees. Thy Kingdom Come. Glory, glory, alleluia. A sudden rush of blood to the head. And … cold-blooded murder. This has its uses as far as my kind are concerned.

I note, though, that before that happens Elijah piles wood upon the altar and drenches it with water. When fire falls from Up There and consumes it, then the penny drops for the onlookers. Tug is God. Drenched wood that reveals God: please observe that textual detail closely. We will return to it.

---

18 1 Kings 18.40.

# Interlogue

*In the beginning was the Word, and the Word was with God, and the Word was God. He was in the beginning with God. All things came into being through him, and without him not one thing came into being. What has come into being in him was life, and the life was the light of all people. The light shines in the darkness, and the darkness did not overcome it.*

*There was a man sent from God, whose name was John. He came as a witness to testify to the light, so that all might believe through him. He himself was not the light, but he came to testify to the light. The true light, which enlightens everyone, was coming into the world.*

*He was in the world, and the world came into being through him; yet the world did not know him. He came to what was his own, and his own people did not accept him. But to all who received him, who believed in his name, he gave power to become children of God, who were born, not of blood or of the will of the flesh or of the will of man, but of God.*

*And the Word became flesh and lived among us, and we have seen his glory, the glory as of a father's only son, full of grace and truth.*

*John 1.1–14*

The remaining episodes of our history are drawn from what the Christians like to think of as 'Part Two' of their 'bible'. Whether they are right to think of this as 'Part Two' of an overarching whole, rather than a loose collection of written ramblings piggybacking onto another loose collection of written ramblings rather depends on one's starting point. Where one was born, when one was born, and so on. Whatever one's starting point, a key question about our history arises at the point where we begin to study what the Christians call their 'Gospels'. They insist on calling the landscape in which we now find ourselves 'New' as opposed to 'Old'. But are they right? Has anything really changed?

I would argue: No, it has not. And I would argue: Yes, it has. For everything has changed. And nothing has changed.

Change, you see, is not one of Tug's great hallmarks. She doesn't go in for it. The Christians bang on and on about this in some of their dullest hymns. She's immortal, she's invisible, she's hid in light inaccessible, et cetera, et cetera. Yawn. But you get the picture. Tug doesn't change. Ever. She's God not a god (Ararat); she doesn't require the blood of the blameless to be spilt (Moriah); she's the air they breathe and the sea in which they swim (Horeb); she's all about 'freedom' (Sinai). By now you know the drill. None of this ever changes. It was, it is, it will be. And ever hereafter. Ad nauseam, you might think. Or even unto the ages of ages ...

Now: were my kind to be lumbered with such changelessness it would be inconvenient. Desperately inconvenient. I mean, it's so much more ... fruitful ... to be able to say one thing to one person and another thing to another, to sway one way one day and another the next, to hold one view this morning and another this afternoon. That's how one gets things done. Change is our department. Very definitely not Tug's.

So in one sense there's nothing remotely 'New' about 'Part Two'. Tug is exactly the same as she always was. But. But, but, but … That's not the whole of it. Because there's a change, too. Not in Tug. As we've established, Tug is unchangeable. But is there a change in what we might call Tug's MO? In her modus operandi? In how she chooses to deal with the humans? In what she elects to show them of Tugself? Yes. I think we can admit that much. To that extent there is what we might call a development.

Think about everything we've learned about Tug: Ararat, Moriah, Horeb, Sinai, Zion, Carmel. Every mountain top. Every encounter. Every last bit of our learning. Every last thing we know of Tug. Now … condense all of it. Every last bit. Give it a human form. Give it a human voice. Give it a human presence. Make it walk and talk. Make it think and act. Make it, make it … be.

Allow me to present … Tug. At least, allow me to present … Tug's Christ-person. Born in Palestine. Born approximately two thousand years ago. Allegedly a descendant of Good King David (remember the family tree nonsense? See above: Mount Zion). This is a notion that the Christians don't press too far as it creates all sorts of difficulties in the doctrinal department. Born in the era when the self-obsessed Romans were busy ordering the world in their image. Raised in Galilee. Probably taught a carpenter's trade. And then … well, that's our next chapter. We'll meet him aged thirty (or thereabouts). We'll meet him in the desert. And (this is where it gets confusing) we'll meet him as he is contemplating Tug's purposes.

Tug. Tug's Christ-person. They're one and the same. That's what's new. Not Tug. Tug's as old as the hills. Older. But Tug in the Christ-person, Tug as the Christ-person, Tug walking, talking, breathing, existing? That's new. Really new. And with the new, with the Christ-person turning up, to quote the humans: Hell-town, we have a problem.

# The Mount of Temptation

*Then Jesus was led up by the Spirit into the wilderness to be tempted by the devil. He fasted for forty days and forty nights, and afterwards he was famished. The tempter came and said to him, 'If you are the Son of God, command these stones to become loaves of bread.' But he answered, 'It is written,*

*"One does not live by bread alone,*
*but by every word that comes from the mouth of God."'*

*Then the devil took him to the holy city and placed him on the pinnacle of the temple, saying to him, 'If you are the Son of God, throw yourself down; for it is written,*

*"He will command his angels concerning you,"*
*and "On their hands they will bear you up,*
*so that you will not dash your foot against a stone."'*

*Jesus said to him, 'Again it is written, "Do not put the Lord your God to the test."'*

*Again, the devil took him to a very high mountain and showed him all the kingdoms of the world and their splendour; and he said to him, 'All these I will give you, if you will fall down and worship me.' Jesus said to him, 'Away with you, Satan! for it is written,*

*"Worship the Lord your God,*
*and serve only him."'*

*Then the devil left him, and suddenly angels came and waited on him.*

*Matthew 4.1–11*

The Chief gets in quickly. Tries to nip 'Part Two' in the bud. Tries to derail the Christ-person before he's found his feet, before he's put in much of an appearance, before he does too much damage.

It doesn't work, of course. It's not the Christ-person who's sent packing. It's the Chief. So there's no glory for my kind here. But it's worth telling the tale.

I believe I have mentioned the ill-starred day when the Chief summoned us and we declared ourselves against Tug and against all Tug's works. Well, the Chief picked up a thing or two that day. It's no good confronting Tug outright. It's no good challenging Tug to feats of strength. It's no good crossing swords with Tug. Tug will always win. No. Our task is to be a little more … creative. A little more circumspect. A little more changeable.

Which is precisely what the Chief is here. Two things. First, he has an inkling of what the Christ-person is all about. He knows that what we're dealing with here is one of the humans. (That's the point. The Christ-person is Tug; the Christ-person is also a human.) Second, the Chief knows the humans. Knows their vanities. Knows their foibles. Knows their proclivities. The Christ-person is one of them. So the Chief puts all that knowledge to work …

The Christ-person heads into the desert. It's as hot as Hell and almost as dull: rocks, dust, lizards. No one to talk to (although the lizards would, frankly, make rather more interesting conversation partners than most of the Galilean villagers among whom he has grown up). Scorching heat and icy cold in monotonous succession. All in all, enough to send the average human round the bend. (Perhaps, if I may make so bold, the Chief should have spotted that and drawn a conclusion about the not-very-averageness of this particular human? Anyway.)

The Christ-person is hungry, exhausted and alone. Enter the Chief. On approaching the Christ-person he activates a three-part stratagem. Masterful. Brilliant. Based upon his profound knowledge of the humans. Following the science, as they say.

1 It is well known that the humans, particularly the males among them, derive most of their motivation from two sets of physical stimuli. One is connected to their seemingly irrepressible urge to procreate. Why they should wish to procreate is mysterious indeed. I mean, wish to produce even more of themselves. Really? The other is connected to the grossness of their digestive appetites. 'Their god is the belly,' writes Saul of Tarsus (him again) in the bible,[19] and, not unusually (I fear), he is right. Think of the hapless Esau and that fateful dish of stew. By and large if you wave a sausage under their noses, you've got them. So. The Christ-person is hungry. 'Command these stones to become loaves of bread,' teases the Chief.

2 Next, every historical record indicates that the humans have an insatiable interest in fame. If that's

19 Philippians 3.19.

not available they'll take notoriety. Whatever. They adore it. They pore over tales of the famous. They long to *be* famous. If they don't wish it for themselves then they wish it for their wretched offspring. Famous for what doesn't matter: famous for kicking a leather ball around, famous for having particular physical proportions, famous for inventing a moon-rocket, famous for … being famous. Who cares? It's the status and the effect of the status that matters. So. The Christ-person is a Galilean nobody. How is he ever going to pull a crowd? Up to the Temple pinnacle he goes. And 'Throw yourself down,' suggests the Chief.

3 Lastly, as food and fame have not worked, the Chief goes for broke. Wealth and power. What human can resist them? With wealth and power come food and fame – more sausages than anyone could ever eat and limitless opportunities for seizing the spotlight. What's not to like? So. The Chief conjures up the kingdoms of the world and all their splendour. 'All these I will give you,' he states.

What was he hoping to achieve? Just this: to knock the Christ-person off course; to spike his guns before he's had a chance to load them and take aim; *to persuade him to take note of a voice that is not Tug's.*

And it fails. Roundly. One can be wise after the event and note that the Christ-person was on top of his game at this point, despite his immediate physical weakness. He had yet to encounter the full extent of the humans' cruelty. He had yet to know bitter failure. He had yet to meet betrayal and treachery. On the contrary, he had his whole life stretching before him and his confidence in Tug, who he is *and* who he calls 'Father' (do not think too hard about this – it is enough of a brain-twister to make even a demon's head ache), was at its peak. Perhaps the Chief could have timed it better and waited for one of the other mountain tops that we will encounter.

However, this is when he chooses to strike. I'd be prepared to wager eternity that there's no other human in history who would have responded as did the Christ-person. Any other human – *any* other human – would have been helpless before the Chief's devilry. But the Christ-person blunts every prong of his pitchfork. Food? No! Fame? No! Wealth and power? No!

Why 'no'? Because at every turn Tug matters more to the Christ-person than does stomach or ego or vanity. It's not that the Christ-person is not (for example) hungry. He is! But it's as though in the Christ-person humanity is perfectly aligned with divinity. The former follows the latter. The Christ-person is hungry – but what would Tug want? The Christ-person could make (good) use of fame – but what would Tug want? The Christ-person looks at wealth and power – and asks, what would Tug want? Incredible. The Christ-person is untouched and untouchable by the most potent temptation and the most skilful tempter that history has known. The Christ-person goes on his way, buoyed up by the encounter and ready to begin Tug's work.

Luckily for us, as I have already noted, no other human would have responded as did the Christ-person, and no other human ever has. The Chief's trident of temptations remains classic textbook stuff. Distract the humans; blow them off course. Get them hooked on satisfying their bodily needs, or fantasizing about celebrity, or acquiring money and influence. It's not that we have actually to deliver any of those – the mere thought is often enough.

It was in a barren place, all rocks and dirt, that Tug's presence was so decisively revealed. No trees for shelter, and no wood for fuel. You might like to remember that.

# The Mount of Teaching

*When Jesus saw the crowds, he went up the mountain; and after he sat down, his disciples came to him. Then he began to speak, and taught them, saying:*

*'Blessed are the poor in spirit, for theirs is the kingdom of heaven.*

*'Blessed are those who mourn, for they will be comforted.*

*'Blessed are the meek, for they will inherit the earth.*

*'Blessed are those who hunger and thirst for righteousness, for they will be filled.*

*'Blessed are the merciful, for they will receive mercy.*

*'Blessed are the pure in heart, for they will see God.*

*'Blessed are the peacemakers, for they will be called children of God.*

*'Blessed are those who are persecuted for righteousness' sake, for theirs is the kingdom of heaven.*

*'Blessed are you when people revile you and persecute you and utter all kinds of evil against you falsely on my account. Rejoice and be glad, for your reward is great in heaven, for in the same way they persecuted the prophets who were before you.'*

*Matthew 5.1–12*

Before you embark upon your study of this mountain top you may wish to refresh your memory of another: Sinai. There's a pleasing parallel between that peak and this. Let me elucidate.

What happens atop Mount Sinai?

Moses goes up the mountain. Moses meets Tug face-to-face. Moses emerges with Tug's words (the 'ten commandments'). Tug's words are neatly inscribed on tablets of stone.

What happens atop the Mount of Teaching?

The humans go up the mountain. The humans meet Tug's Christ-person face-to-face. The humans emerge with his words ('the beatitudes'). But ... no tablets of stone. Not this time. Instead, his words are neatly inserted into the humans' ears. And etched upon their minds. And inscribed on their hearts.

Our preliminary conclusion from this neat parallel? That the Christ-person is Moses. At least, he's not Moses. He's from the same stable as Moses. He's the successor to Moses. As it were.

It couldn't be clearer. It might as well have been carved into some of those stone tablets that Tug used to favour.

As infants both Moses and the Christ-person are laid in rather unlikely receptacles. The former? A basket smeared with tar and pushed out among the bulrushes[20] (think of the trouble we'd have been saved if an enterprising crocodile

20 Exodus 2.1–10.

had holed it beneath the waterline). The latter? An animal's feeding trough in a stable behind a Bethlehem inn.[21]

As infants both Moses and the Christ-person come out of Egypt to the land Tug has given their people. Moses, fleeing a tyrannical despot *from* Egypt; the Christ-person, fleeing a tyrannical despot *to* Egypt.[22]

And then, and then … mountain tops, meetings … and words. Divine words.

Conclusion? The Christ-person stands where Moses once stood. QED.

Which means what? Moses was Tug's appointee; Moses was the leader of Tug's people; Moses was the mediator between Tug's people and Tug; Moses was the great liberator. And now? It's the Christ-person who is all those things. He is the leader, the mediator and the liberator. More 'anointed' than 'appointed', I grant you, but you get the picture.

But there's more. For as this mountain top indicates, the Christ-person is also … the teacher. And here there are some little signs of hope.

You see, not all the Christians are terminally stupid. Not all. It takes them a while, but they eventually work out what has been plain as a cloven hoof all along. The Christ-person is not just Moses. He's not even just Moses on stilts. No. As we have already established, in the Christ-person all Tug's power, all Tug's glory and all Tug's presence dwell. The Christ-person is not just a teacher of 'Good News'. Tug's

---

21 Luke 2.1–7.
22 Matthew 2.19–23.

Christ-person is the 'Good News'. But this remarkable discovery has an unintended consequence.

When the Christians work out who the Christ-person is (see above) they really get to work. Creeds are written to explain him; paintings are created to glorify him; statues are carved to immortalize him; prayers are crafted to offer to him; praises are wafted before him; titles are composed and lavished upon him. All very understandable and to some extent very laudable. Doctrine a gogo. The Christians have cracked it, and they want everyone else to know that they've cracked it. The Second Person of their Trinity has landed. Hurrah!

But what about what the Christ-person said and how the Christ-person lived? What about the dusty highways of Galilee and the forgotten synagogues of Nazareth and Capernaum? Ah! The Christians are less insistent about all of those. The thing is that the Christ-person is Tug and Tug is the Christ-person. The beginning of his life is important (see above: that dratted stable). So too is the 'end' of his life (another mountain top, Golgotha, to which we'll come).

Which leaves the beatitudes and a lot of other stuff. The Christians read it all, of course, but how much notice do they take of it? By and large, very little. Because the Christ-person's teaching is ... To me it's downright preposterous. But to the Christians? It's hard, just hard, very hard. It's easy to sing songs about how marvellous the Christ-person is and easy to profess lifelong attachment to, indeed infatuation with, him. But living as he lives, making the choices he makes? They're less enthusiastic about that. You see, read those beatitudes. They're not straightforward.

They're not a guide to how a Christian should act. They're a guide to what a Christian should be. That's tricky.

I only said that not all the Christians were terminally stupid. Press most of them on what they regard as his teaching for how they should live, and where do they look? To Moses and those ten commandments. It's old hat but it's true. The commandments are much more easily digestible by the humans than are the beatitudes. They have straightforward instructions and straightforward injunctions. 'No' to stealing; 'no' to sleeping with a neighbour's spouse; 'no' to falsehoods. And so on. A lot of the Christians can probably look at themselves in the mirror and think, 'Well, I've pretty much kept the majority of those.'

It would be difficult for many of them to make the same claim about the beatitudes. Poor in spirit? Hungry and thirsty for righteousness? Pure in heart? Don't make me laugh. The Christians can just about cope with rules and regulations. But the Mount of Teaching? It's in a different league.

What they mostly fail to grasp is that it's impossible for them to live as the beatitudes direct without a bit of help. Most of them can get through the day without actually stealing anything or murdering anyone. But purity of heart, or meekness, or mercy are not things they can tick off as accomplished by lunchtime. No. They are a lifetime's work and – to be blunt – they are the Christ-person's work *in them*, not theirs *on the Christ-person's behalf.*

The Christ-person wants more for them than they can possibly hope to achieve for themselves. If they would only stop being so busily virtuous, so stuck on rules and regulations, so hell-bent (see what I did there?) on working out their own salvation they might discover that he's alive and well … and, as they say, closer to them than they are to themselves. That's the deal.

The Christ-person doesn't dwell in temples or churches. He dwells in the hearts of faithful humans (remember: the beatitudes weren't carved on stone tablets). If they'll let him, he's willing to transform them beyond recognition, one by one, little by little, making their ghastly little lives showplaces for everything he/Tug ever spoke about. They will become poor in spirit, hungry for righteousness etc. etc. Slowly, incrementally, but inexorably. They just need to shut up, clear out of his way, and let him get on with it.

Thankfully, they are terrible at that. They think they know so much better …

# Mount Tabor

*Now about eight days after these sayings Jesus took with him Peter and John and James, and went up on the mountain to pray. And while he was praying, the appearance of his face changed, and his clothes became dazzling white. Suddenly they saw two men, Moses and Elijah, talking to him. They appeared in glory and were speaking of his departure, which he was about to accomplish at Jerusalem. Now Peter and his companions were weighed down with sleep; but since they had stayed awake, they saw his glory and the two men who stood with him. Just as they were leaving him, Peter said to Jesus, 'Master, it is good for us to be here; let us make three dwellings, one for you, one for Moses, and one for Elijah' – not knowing what he said. While he was saying this, a cloud came and overshadowed them; and they were terrified as they entered the cloud. Then from the cloud came a voice that said, 'This is my Son, my Chosen; listen to him!' When the voice had spoken, Jesus was found alone. And they kept silent and in those days told no one any of the things they had seen.*

*Luke 9.28–36*

Had I – had any of my kind – been present, then what transpired here would have had us howling in agony for all eternity.

The mountain top is never named, which matters not one jot – except that, for some of the Christians, it does. It matters several pages, full of jots. This sort of Christian obsesses over geographical particularity (indeed, all sorts of particularity), which has allowed this sort to concentrate on claiming land, defining boundaries, falling out with other Christians, and all manner of behaviour guaranteed not to impress Tug. This is invariably helpful to my kind. But I digress: there's a general consensus that the mountain we're talking about here is Mount Tabor.

So – up Mount Tabor trudge the Christ-person and the Talentless Trio. Dull-witted Peter, James and little John must have been thoroughly pleased with themselves. Hand-picked by Teacher for this special Sunday School outing which leaves the other nine waiting on the bus. Well: the Trio certainly get more than they were bargaining for (and, as we shall see, they fail quite spectacularly to rise to the occasion).

For up at the summit, as the Christ-person prays, the veil that separates Heaven from Earth is pulled aside. If that sounds uncharacteristically poetic then I apologize, but there really is no other way to describe it. Light streams forth from him, light of a brightness unseen since the day of creation, light that would have scorched my deathless eyes had I looked upon it. And a voice speaks from a cloud. Now: Tug has always been keen on clouds (think Sinai). The voice could only be Tug's voice, a voice that would have made my blood run cold (had any blood run through my bloodless veins).

And what do you know? Our old acquaintances Moses

and Elijah put in special guest appearances. Moses has evidently calmed down since our last, stone-flinging, encounter; Elijah has had the good grace to wash the blood of the prophets from his hands. There they stand, deep in conversation with the Christ-person, gloating. Except that I bet they don't. The Christ-person doesn't gloat. Tug doesn't gloat.

There's no mistaking what's going on. It's a land grab. Or, a land re-grab. Heaven has unfurled its banner and planted it firmly on Earth. Tug is making a statement: this is her world. Her glory extends to its farthest corner; she is sovereign over it, over all of it. Hers is ultimately the only show in town.

This has consequences for the likes of me. My kind cannot hope to challenge her directly. After all – as you may recall – these notes began when the Chief declared all-out war and summoned up siege engines against Heaven's battlements. We know how that ended. No. The task facing us is far more subtle than many of us have hitherto believed. It is that of guerrillas and saboteurs. It is to knock the humans off course and tantalize their ears (see above: Mount of Temptation). It is to keep the humans from seeing what was revealed on the peak of Mount Tabor. It is to keep them from seeing that Tug is all and is in all. It is to keep them from seeing that the Earth – their home – is the place where Tug's Kingdom is being realized. It is to keep them from seeing that Tug is at their fingertips, in the room with them, closer to them than they are to themselves (see above: Mount of Teaching). It is to keep the humans' heads down, to keep them fixated on their passing needs, on their trivial obsessions and on their abstract speculations. It is these that are supremely important.

Peter is a splendid example. What a gift to the cause. On Mount Tabor he is confronted by the Lord of Glory in all his awesome majesty. Goodness me (as it were), Peter has come a long way from scratching a living in a fishing boat off Capernaum. From Tilapia to Tabor! Now, Peter sees Heaven's light glowing on a mountain top; he hears the voice from the cloud; he sees Moses and Elijah, characters he's been hearing stories about since he was knee-high to a mackerel. He actually sees them.

And how does our doughty hero respond? He offers to build a shed. Permit me to repeat that. He offers to build a shed. You couldn't make it up.

I've already had something to say about human vulnerability among the males of that wretched species (Aaron, Esau et al.). Here we see it in all its marvellous crassness. Peter is offered a glimpse of eternity and he thinks only of wooden planks and iron nails. As if wooden planks nailed together could bear the Creator of Earth and Heaven! Actually, please note that detail of the text. It is one to which I will return in the pages that lie ahead.

Peter sees with the eyes of a Galilean peasant. He was certainly well named. 'The Rock'?[23] It's a good assessment of his intellectual capacity. Peter the Fisherman. Thick as granite, but – bless him – always able to turn his hand to anything. So he reverts to type. If in doubt, mend a net. Or fix a boat. Or knock up a shed.

---

23 Matthew 16.18.

But there's a substratum operating here which is extremely valuable. Building a shed isn't just an honest craftsman's honest response to an uncertain situation. It's also a vanity project. It really is. Men and their sheds. Peter wants it to be admired. He wants it to be the best shed in the whole of Galilee!

'Let us make three dwellings,' he blethers. I honestly think he wants Tug to notice. I think he wants his thanks. 'A shed?' Peter probably imagines him saying. 'What a shed! A beautiful shed! A well-appointed shed! What a stunning work of craftsmanship! Thank you, Peter! Have an especially glittery halo!'

It is insufferably vain – Peter is insufferably vain. But can you see what has happened? In the face of the most extravagant outpouring of glory that the humans have ever seen, Peter has been completely captivated by his own emotional neediness. He exchanged the glory of the immortal God for a wooden shed, as Saul of Tarsus (I know, I know) might have written.[24] How utterly wonderful. You give me hope, Peter. You set before my kind the pattern of our calling. When Tug unfurls his banner so unmistakably you ignore the splendour, you ignore the glory, you ignore the mystery. You ignore Tug. Thankfully you set a pattern that many are willing to copy.

24 Romans 1.23.

# The Mount of Olives

*Then Jesus went with them to a place called Gethsemane; and he said to his disciples, 'Sit here while I go over there and pray.' He took with him Peter and the two sons of Zebedee, and began to be grieved and agitated. Then he said to them, 'I am deeply grieved, even to death; remain here, and stay awake with me.' And going a little farther, he threw himself on the ground and prayed, 'My Father, if it is possible, let this cup pass from me; yet not what I want but what you want.' Then he came to the disciples and found them sleeping; and he said to Peter, 'So, could you not stay awake with me one hour? Stay awake and pray that you may not come into the time of trial; the spirit indeed is willing, but the flesh is weak.' Again he went away for the second time and prayed, 'My Father, if this cannot pass unless I drink it, your will be done.' Again he came and found them sleeping, for their eyes were heavy. So leaving them again, he went away and prayed for the third time, saying the same words. Then he came to the disciples and said to them, 'Are you still sleeping and taking your rest? See, the hour is at hand, and the Son of Man is betrayed into the hands of sinners. Get up, let us be going. See, my betrayer is at hand.'*

*Matthew 26.36–46*

The Christ-person wavers. 'My Father, if it is possible, let this cup pass from me.' Then he makes up his mind. 'Yet not what I want but what you want.' The die is cast; the Rubicon is crossed; the goose is cooked.

We have reached the Mount of Olives. Olivet. Strategically positioned, overlooking Jerusalem and Tug's Temple, roughly adjacent to Mount Zion and to the ancient stomping ground (or should that be romping ground?) of King David.

Anyway: Olivet. The Christ-person likes it here. After a good dinner, the lofty altitude and the leafy shade offer a welcome respite from the heat and noise of the city. He and his cronies have just enjoyed a good dinner. They have been here often. Which is why Judas knows where to find him.

Oh, Judas. Poor, pitiful, pathetic lout. The son of Simon Iscariot. The gallons of ink, the lungfuls of breath, the industrial quantities of energy that have been expended on the miserable little toad.

Look: Judas has not been without his uses as far as my kind are concerned. We may smile at the heights of self-righteous indignation to which he has propelled the Christians, monumental even by their stratospheric standards. We may relish the waves of dishonest defamation and cruel persecution that Judas' treachery has allowed them to unleash on others. This has been thrillingly vicious. We may applaud the blindness to their own shortcomings that all this has induced in them. They bang on about Judas' motives, telling themselves: perhaps it was – greed. Those pieces of silver might have gone a long way in the dirt-poor world that Judas inhabited. Perhaps it was – disillusionment. The great revolt had not materialized. No slitting of Roman throats; no public lynching of collaborators; no lining of the comrades' pockets (i.e. none of the usual things that human revolutionaries tend to go in for). Or perhaps it was – desperation. The hope that placing the Christ-person in imminent danger would compel him/Tug to act. 'Arrest, trial, execution? Uh-oh. Better summon the legions of angels …'

Perhaps it was all of these. Perhaps it was none of them. The significant point to note is that with J. Iscariot carrying the can the Christians have been provided with yet another ready-made excuse for overlooking their own greed, their own disillusionment and their own desperate readiness to throw the innocent under the bus. But I digress. Again.

I suppose I hoped that even at this stage the Christ-person might falter. Might run away, his tail between his legs, anxious to avoid the fate that is about to consume him. At least three considerations favoured such an outcome. First, there was the lateness of the hour and that supper that he had eaten. Bodily and mental fatigue and a glass or two of wine are very considerable allies in the war against virtue. Weary and worse-for-wear, the humans will do almost anything.

Second, there was his utter isolation. Yet again, Peter and the rest of the menagerie of losers, half-wits and ne'er do-wells prove themselves about as useful as a pair of chocolate manacles in Gehenna's hottest pit. He pleads with them to stay awake and watch with him. You would think it wouldn't be too much to ask, wouldn't you? Well, in the face of their world-beating mediocrity you'd be wrong.

And third, there was the thought of everything he might achieve were he simply to slip into the shadows and hotfoot it back to Galilee. He could have done so. Trees and bushes aplenty; a dark night; a hillside that he knew well. The Christ-person could have been halfway to Nazareth by the time Judas turns up in the garden. No arrest, no trial, no execution.

But the Christ-person stays. He waits. It's a bit ironic. He begins his career surrounded by the wood shavings of a carpenter's shop. He ends it surrounded by the wood of an olive grove. On Mount Tabor, Peter, peerless fixer of wooden boats, offers to knock up a shed to contain the divine presence. On Mount Horeb the dry twigs of the burning bush crackle and disclose the divine radiance. On Mount Ararat the cypress wood of the ark stands high above the flood waters and bears the divine promise. Now on the Mount of Olives, the wood of the trees might have concealed the divine person from his pursuers. But. But, but, but … I've said a few times that we will return to the subject in the course of these notes. And now it is time for us to do so.

Isaac walks towards Mount Moriah bearing on his back the wood on which he is to die. And Tug puts a stop to it. The Christ-person walks from the Mount of Olives towards another hilltop bearing on his back the wood on which he is to die. And Tug does nothing about it. In fact, Tug urges him on. As it were.

Why?

The boy Isaac knows nothing of what awaits him. He is what the humans might call a helpless innocent. Moriah teaches us that Tug doesn't require that the blood of the blameless should be spilled. Tug doesn't require the smoke and fuss of their sacrifices. He most certainly doesn't require them to start sacrificing each other.

The Christ-person is not Isaac. He is every bit as innocent as the boy, true, but he walks towards his fate, bearing his cross, knowing exactly what awaits him. He chooses not to avoid it, deny it or resist it.

It isn't that the Christ-person wants to die. He is one of the ludicrous humans, after all. He has their natural aversion to pain and death. He doesn't want to suffer (see above: the die, the Rubicon, the goose).

But – this is important – he does want to be faithful. In fact, he has to be faithful. Faithful is who he is. Faithful is what he does. The Christ-person remains faithful to Tug's will. Which is the Christ-person's will. As it were. Confusing, I know. But this is why Judas Iscariot is ultimately irrelevant. The Christ-person's faithfulness means that he was never going anywhere that Thursday night. He would have stayed on Olivet whether JI had shown up or not. Really.

Suppose Judas had done a bunk? Suppose he had had a sudden attack of remorse? Suppose he had gone back to the Temple and told old Caiaphas to sling his hook? Say he had slunk off into the night? The Christ-person would have been back at the Temple the next day, doing his thing, making himself visible, rendering himself vulnerable. And the next day. And the day after. He would have gone on and on, doing what he did – that's what faithfulness means. And no doubt eventually someone would have stopped him. If not Judas then some other hapless fall-guy.

The Christ-person does not run away. He does not fight back. He stays faithful, faithful in the face of the torrent of torture, scorn and poison that is about to engulf him. I am going to stick my neck out now. I don't mind admitting: isn't there something – something almost admirable – about him?

# Golgotha

*Then they brought Jesus to the place called Golgotha (which means the place of a skull). And they offered him wine mixed with myrrh; but he did not take it. And they crucified him, and divided his clothes among them, casting lots to decide what each should take.*

*It was nine o'clock in the morning when they crucified him. The inscription of the charge against him read, 'The King of the Jews.' And with him they crucified two bandits, one on his right and one on his left. Those who passed by derided him, shaking their heads and saying, 'Aha! You who would destroy the temple and build it in three days, save yourself, and come down from the cross!' In the same way the chief priests, along with the scribes, were also mocking him among themselves and saying, 'He saved others; he cannot save himself. Let the Messiah, the King of Israel, come down from the cross now, so that we may see and believe.' Those who were crucified with him also taunted him.*

*When it was noon, darkness came over the whole land until three in the afternoon. At three o'clock Jesus cried out with a loud voice, 'Eloi, Eloi, lema sabachthani?' which means, 'My God, my God, why have you forsaken me?' When some of the bystanders heard it, they said,*

*'Listen, he is calling for Elijah.' And someone ran, filled a sponge with sour wine, put it on a stick, and gave it to him to drink, saying, 'Wait, let us see whether Elijah will come to take him down.' Then Jesus gave a loud cry and breathed his last.*

*Mark 15.22–37*

Arguably, this is not a hilltop at all. And it's certainly not green, despite all the tedious hymn-writing of the wretched Christians (I'm honestly not obsessed with this particular topic). It is a limestone quarry outside one of Jerusalem's gates, unmentioned by the bible's diarists and chroniclers until this point. None of the various miscreants who have filled our pages are recorded as whiling away the hours with a saunter along Golgotha's sun-kissed heights. Unsurprising. It does not have any.

The ambience of Golgotha is bizarrely calculated to appeal to my rebel sensibilities. 'Utterly desolate, Golgotha is lavishly decked with human blood, generously ornamented with human sweat and lovingly anointed with human excrement; its rank breezes are perfumed with the sweet odour of death; its air sings with music made by those who hang in agony and by the birds of prey that feast on their putrefying corpses.' Had I had the extreme misfortune to be born a human I could have become one of their estate agents!

Golgotha is hellish. But ultimately that makes no difference to what happens there. For we have reached the hour of the Chief's defeat – of my kind's defeat. Complete and utter. Total. Yes, we were defeated on the plains of Heaven on that far-off inglorious day when we were thrown down. But that was as nothing compared to this.

For him, it doesn't look like a victory. That much I'll allow. The Christ-person's tortured frame is nailed to the woodwork. He gasps desperately for every breath. His blood congeals around his gaping wounds. It's the punishment reserved for slaves and traitors. Over the centuries the humans have proved themselves remarkably adept at devising ingenious ways to kill each other. Not many trump this. It looks like he was beaten.

It's what happens when the heavenly faithfulness that we saw atop the Mount of Olives is released into the world that the humans inhabit. The Christ-person turns up. The Christ-person sticks around. The Christ-person is faithful to Tug's will (which is the Christ-person's will). And what happens? Golgotha happens.

The divine faithfulness runs headlong into the maelstrom of violence and terror that is the humans' meat and drink. Faithfulness meets insecure power; faithfulness meets unaccountable rage; faithfulness meets crippling fear. Power, rage and fear unite in an all-conquering phalanx and sweep the Christ-person away. Nail him to a cross.

He dies. He … dies.

And, for a while, that's enough. The Christ-person was evidently not the one for whom so many of the gullible idiots had been waiting. There had been no calling Israel to arms, no glorious advances on the Roman legions and no Coming of the Kingdom. Instead, there had been Golgotha

– dice thrown for his tattered rags and a gibbet hammered into the rock between two thugs. Why would anyone fix their hope on one who had come to so ignoble an end?

But it didn't take long for one or two bright sparks to cotton on to the obscene truth. Golgotha was not Tug's defeat. Golgotha was Tug's eternal victory.

I believe we have come across the insufferable Saul of Tarsus before? More than once. He summed this up in his typically lofty assertion that what looks like foolishness to the humans looks like wisdom to Tug.[25] You see, Saul and his gang worked out what my kind had known all along. The Christ-person commends his soul to his Father and breathes his last. The humans have immersed him in the toxic vomit of their violence and terror. Yet he has remained faithful. He has not hit back.

And his faithfulness meant that human violence and human terror had no power over him – that death itself had no power over him. He refused to hold anyone captive. Quid pro quo: he could not be held captive. 'It is accomplished,' he stammers. And 'it' really is. None of my kind will ever forget that day. All Hell broke loose in a howling cacophony of rage and grief that overwhelmed even Pandemonium.

But. But, but, but. My kind are down, but not out; beaten, but not eliminated. How might we continue the struggle as elucidated above (Temptation, Tabor etc.)? Let us attempt a strategic approach to this mountain top and to what follows it.

---

25 1 Corinthians 1.18–25.

One tactic is to concentrate the humans' minds on Golgotha, and to do so at the expense of what transpires three days later, in a nearby garden sepulchre. If we insert a very solid and inky full stop into the story of the Christ-person immediately after his death, and then stand well back, some very rewarding results emerge. What happens in the garden sepulchre features only as an afterthought, as something that comes along only when the audience are already putting on their coats and heading for the exit. The full stop after '... and breathed his last' encourages the witless humans to immerse themselves in Golgotha's blood and agony. It encourages them to fill their heads with The Sacrifice Once Offered, with The Price He Paid For Me, with My Suffering Lord (if estate agency doesn't work out perhaps I too could write hymns!). It may thus encourage them to forget the lesson of Ararat and to conceive of Tug as a god: as a fickle god, who changes his mind when he is offered a gift (The Sacrifice); or as an angry god, who demands that blameless blood be spilt on his account (The Price); or as a quasi-human god, who suffers alongside his people (My Suffering Lord). See? Any of these conceptions (or misconceptions) on the part of the humans is immensely advantageous.

The opposite tactic is to downplay Golgotha at the expense of what happens in the garden sepulchre. This is undoubtedly trickier, because many of the dull humans get a bit embarrassed about the empty tomb. They may adore crystals; they may be mad about reincarnation; they may sign up for poltergeists, spells and fortune-telling. But resurrection? Umm ... To me it's simple: of course the tomb is empty and of course the Christ-person is raised.

He must be raised, because Tug lives eternally. It's one of those things we teach young rebels before they can wield a toasting-fork. But to the pedestrian human mind it is not simple. Not at all. 'How can the resurrection be proved?' they are likely to bleat. Getting them to focus on the plain fact of what happens in the garden sepulchre may be tricky.

So a sub-tactic is to get them to home in on it as a lovely idea, an attractive notion, a metaphor. Thus: '… never mind those ancient stories about a rolling stone and angels[26] and the road to Emmaus.[27] It's what the stories represent that matters: the triumph of faithfulness, the persistence of friendship, the vindication of the everlasting Human Spirit' etc. etc. A lot of 'sophisticated' humans (ha!) will fall for this line, and then it's an easy step to get them to dismiss the crucifixion as a relic of some early, primitive, sub-Christian religion. And then the battle is all but won! They will have a religion, all right, but it will be pink and fluffy. They will imagine that come what may, somehow, one day, they will fly away to be with their Tuggy. Jam yesterday, jam today, jam tomorrow, and jam for the whole of eternity. Sweet, sticky, sickly – and stupid. No sin, no death, no judgement, no wrinkles to crease the counterpane of their untroubled lives, just Tuggy, as comfortable and reassuring as an 18 Tog duvet. Or, should I say: an 18 *Tug* duvet?

And if all else fails, one last tactic is to persuade the humans that, whatever their view of Golgotha and the garden sepulchre, those events happened only once, and they happened a very long time ago. They are to be

26 Matthew 28.2.

27 Luke 24.13–35.

honoured, or they are to be discounted. Take your pick! An effective line may be: 'Did it happen? Did it not happen? It's really your choice – whatever works for you.' The serious business of living today can then be got on with. There may be connections to be drawn between that serious business and those far-off events in first-century Palestine. Or there may not. They are ancient history. Or sentimental nostalgia. You choose. But they have no bearing upon the present.

Three suggestions. The journey is almost at an end.

# The Mount of Ascension

> *So when they had come together, they asked him, 'Lord, is this the time when you will restore the kingdom to Israel?' He replied, 'It is not for you to know the times or periods that the Father has set by his own authority. But you will receive power when the Holy Spirit has come upon you; and you will be my witnesses in Jerusalem, in all Judea and Samaria, and to the ends of the earth.' When he had said this, as they were watching, he was lifted up, and a cloud took him out of their sight. While he was going and they were gazing up towards heaven, suddenly two men in white robes stood by them. They said, 'Men of Galilee, why do you stand looking up towards heaven? This Jesus, who has been taken up from you into heaven, will come in the same way as you saw him go into heaven.'*
>
> *Acts 1.6–11*

Relocation. I suppose it's one way of describing what happened to the Chief after our heroic sortie against Tug and his ultra-angelic toadies. An enforced relocation. Relocation is something the humans are awfully keen on – relocating their homes, relocating their businesses, relocating their burdensome elderly relatives – all in the mistaken belief that this will improve their rotten lives. It makes heaps of cash for those estate agents I've mentioned.

Anyhow. This mountain top is about a relocation. Or is it?

Perhaps, at this stage of the journey, geographical detail does not matter. We may be back on the Mount of Olives. We may be somewhere else. Whatever. The still-sheepish fan-club cluster around the evidently-no-longer-dead Christ-person. I console myself with the thought that Peter et al. must have been feeling particularly stupid. The Christ-person speaks some words of comfort. And then? He goes. Relocates. And the credulous morons are left gazing up into the sky.

Where does he go? I repeat: where does he go?

You see, from this moment on the precise location of the Christ-person becomes a source of embarrassment and confusion for those of the Christians who have stuck with the programme. And thus it becomes a source of tactical advantage.

We begin with the bible. As you will note, 'Luke' (scribbler of 'Acts' as well as of the imaginatively entitled 'Luke') has a crack at describing what happens on this mountain top. Always something of a poet, he reaches for language about clouds, about white-robed men, and about the Christ-person being 'lifted up'.

It is, if I may say so, a fatal error on 'Luke's' part. It makes it sound as though the Christ-person has left the Earth behind. But has he?

You see: press them on the subject and many of the Christians believe that he has. They believe that Tug is Up There. They believe that the Christ-person is Up There too.

True, they believe that he was Down Here before he returned Up There, before he relocated. But the consequence is that – with unimpeachable logic – they believe that right now they are on their own. Admittedly, Tug stretches out a helping hand every so often, through the agency of the shadowy H. Ghost, Esq. (and this in response to fervent prayer or elaborate ritual). Basically, though, he has left them to get on with a task that he supervises remotely from behind his heavenly desk (albeit relocated to a place they do not understand and cannot describe). They may pay lip-service to the notion that the Christ-person/Tug/H. Ghost will come again. But this will be on some impossibly far-off day in the future that they can barely begin to imagine.

They can thus be persuaded to believe that the Earth is a battleground and that the battle's outcome is yet to be decided. The Christ-person has relocated from it, rendering it a cruel and hostile environment where my kind, malevolent and powerful, lie in wait around every corner, ready to confound the Christians and consume them.

Now, this view of the theatre of operations is extraordinarily helpful. Let the Christians believe that they are alone and at our mercy. But let us be clear: this is their self-deception. It is utter codswallop. Pure bilge. The Earth is not an unresolved battleground. The Earth is Tug's, and he has not abandoned it. As if he ever could or ever would!

The humans really have learned nothing.

In the Christ-person, Tug has won. From the Mount of Temptation to the Place of the Skull it is writ large that the victory is his. Remember the blaze of light that streams from his face on Mount Tabor. Remember the faithfulness which allows him to step calmly into the path of the oncoming juggernaut of hatred on Olivet. And remember what happens in the garden sepulchre, however much it pains you. Nothing can contain or confine him. Nothing in life and nothing in death, nothing in Heaven and nothing in Hell. To suggest otherwise is pure Beelzebullocks.

Tug has not relocated. On Mount Carmel, old Elijah makes his witty jibe that 'gods' like Baal turn their back and wander off. Not gods like God! On Ararat, Tug places a rainbow in the sky and declares that he will never turn against the humans, never, ever again. On Horeb, Tug lets slip that he is Being Itself. On Mount Zion, Good King David, blood-spiller and bed-hopper, becomes one of Tug's greatest pals, with the clear-as-day message that no one is beyond the pale. No one. Ever. After all that, Tug is hardly going to clear off back to Heaven leaving the humans to get on with it, is he?

No. No, no, no. The Divine Relocation (or 'Ascension') does not mean that the Christ-person does the equivalent of setting up shop on an industrial estate in Harlow or nipping out for a quick pint and never getting home for tea. All the history we have just recalled means that Tug cannot but be committed, utterly committed, to the Earth and to the humans. The Christ-person ascends, for crying out loud: he is not Elvis Presley, and when the Christ-person ascends Tug does not leave the building. Tug remains with, among, around the humans. But he can no longer be identified with one pair of feet and one set of hands and one human face. The 'Ascension' means that the Christ-person is liberated; he is exalted; he is glorified; he is … oh, I shall run out of words.

He made this all very clear in those beatitudes (see above: Teaching). Following him is not about doing, it's about being (poor in spirit, hungry for righteousness, etc. etc.). The sort of being that interests him requires him to inhabit the hearts and minds of the humans, to live in them, to change them from within, to transform them so that they will be like him, so that they too will be glorified.

For 'Ascension' is the humans' destiny. 'Glorification' is the humans' destiny. They are made to be like him. But most of them are too pig-ignorant to realize this. Instead, they read 'Luke' as relating a frankly implausible event (the Christ-person zooming up into the starry ether). This they dare not interrogate too closely lest they should transgress the truth of the bible and bring the thought-police down on them like a ton of bricks. Yet their careless reading and amateurish theologizing has the effect of convincing them that they have been left to their own devices, fighting the Chief and his legions single-handed in a world from which the now-enthroned-in-glory Christ-person is pretty well absent (although they can't say where).

Well, let them believe that. As I have noted, the benefits are considerable. And it means our journey can limp to a conclusion on a semi-upbeat note.

But it is time to ask one final question.

Why?

# Epilogue

On Horeb, dry sticks of wood blaze with fire. And … Tug is present.

On Zion, a wooden bedstead creaks with adulterous passion. And … Tug is present.

On Golgotha, a wooden cross is soaked in blood. And … Tug is present.

But why? Why does Tug choose to make Tugself known in these squalid environments? As we observed right at the very beginning, Tug casts the Chief from the crystal battlements of Heaven; he plunges him (and we who follow him) into the abyss of Hell; he commands the earth and the skies above it.

Yet Tug chooses Aaron. And David. And Bathsheba. And Peter. And Judas. Tug is the breath that fills their lungs (Horeb); Tug longs for them to be free (Sinai); Tug forgives their shameless flouting of the most basic of his wishes (Zion). Tug waits for them in Gethsemane; Tug prays for them on Golgotha; Tug's limbs are stretched out by them on the cross, and at their hands his Christ-person suffers the most exquisitely painful death that they've ever devised.

Why?

Why? Why? Why?

I believe that it's because Tug loves the humans.

Just look at them. Aaron's heedless mob dancing themselves dizzy. David leaping into Bathsheba's bed. Peter, Thomas and the other useless clowns fleeing the garden in terror and leaving the Christ-person to die alone. An unending parade of self-centred idiocy, of wanton destructiveness, of emotional, sexual and devotional incontinence. Ghastliness. Where would the humans be if there were any proper justice? A place with which I am rather familiar, that's where. A place where the stink of sulphur clogs the nostrils and endless night kills the soul. A place where the tap-tap-tap of the infernal laptop echoes in everlasting desolation …

But Tug's response to their unmitigated irresponsibility? Their ghastliness is met with his faithfulness. No death-dealing earthquakes. No thunder and lightning. No eternal torment. It's what's been made clear on Horeb, and Sinai, and Zion, and Golgotha. Tug is their God. Tug is the pulse that beats in their blood. Tug has made them to be free. And Tug forgives them.

And why? Because he loves them.

Now then: love. One view is that love is purely illusory, another of the humans' many self-deceptions. It will certainly withstand only limited rational analysis. But it is for dull human minds to get hung up about that. The so-called wisdom of the so-called 'Enlightenment' more or less urges that unless something can be pared back, stripped down and detailed with arithmetical precision it cannot possibly be real. That's why the humans run into difficulties with something as stark staringly obvious as what happens in the garden sepulchre. What happens there is clearly a matter of common sense (Tug is, so naturally death is not. Not ultimately, that is). *Pace* the wisdom of the Enlightenment, the merest glance at the human world convinces even a mottled old sceptic like me that love is real. Nothing else can explain the humans' (and Tug's) otherwise frankly incomprehensible behaviour.

Admitting that love *is* does not equate to understanding it. My kind don't. Can't. But it has been very useful! Useful because it throws up a great deal of froth and a mass of detritus which can very easily be exploited. To what am I referring? Like the fruit of the vine to which the humans are irretrievably drawn (see above: Olivet), love renders the humans blind, deaf and even more lacking in judgement than is their usual condition. So my kind may derive huge pleasure (and tactical benefit) from love's folly, impetuousness and tragedy. My kind may scoff at its vulnerability and its sheer crassness. And my kind may take advantage of the rampant lust that accompanies it, of the impaired judgement that is a casualty of it, and of the super-sized vanity that it seems to encourage in those smitten by it.

Love, as I observe it, is always outgoing. I suppose it must be, or else it's some form of self-gratification. Love seeks the beloved and goes after the beloved. Love is careless of whatever injury or scorn it may endure along the way. And isn't that Tug's modus operandi? The humans forget his name and his nature; they run after shiny idols; they abuse one another and kill one another; they torture, betray and deny all that is dearest to them. And Tug constantly picks them up and allows them another chance. He constantly refuses to take offence at their carelessness, ineptitude and selfishness. He constantly exposes himself to their callousness and stupidity.

Only the reality of love can explain any of this. And only the reality of love can explain the arrival of the Christ-person. I repeat: love seeks the beloved and goes after the beloved. Love is careless of whatever injury or scorn it may endure along the way – Tug's pattern from Ararat onwards.

Now, all of this history of unconditional love is drawn together, summed up, and given a face and voice in the Christ-person. Poor old Moses is enraged on Tug's behalf as he descends Mount Sinai to confront the cavorting mob; but when the Christ-person turns up Tug is now present Tugself, at the sharp end of the mob's taunts, at the tips of their spears, and on the receiving end of their peculiarly nasty habit of crucifixion. So whereas when young Isaac lies on the altar his father somehow manages to tune his cloth-ears into Tug's will and to take notice of what he hears, when the Christ-person lies where Isaac lay the humans show no such restraint. They surround him and bear him away. They chain him and beat him. They spit on him and jeer at him. Down comes the knife (or the nails and the crown of thorns). Love comes into the world, and love is crushed under the weight of the humans' rage, pain and fear.

Except, of course, that it can't be. Love, that is. It can't be crushed. It can't be destroyed. Not by anything. Ever. Which is why the Chief was defeated. And why Tug was not.

Tug's love for them. Constant, unwavering, eternal. That's the only story. That's what this is all about. I rather wish I could draw a more – a more sophisticated conclusion. But I can't.

And perhaps that's my rebel vanity talking. Tug's love. For them. Game, set and match.

How extraordinary that so many of them simply don't believe it. Thank God. As it were.